THE BAD GUYS

EPISODE 7   EPISODE 8

D1335862

Scholastic Children's Books
An imprint of Scholastic Ltd
Euston House, 24 Eversholt Street, London, NW1 1DB, UK
Registered office: Westfield Road, Southam, Warwickshire, CV47 0RA
SCHOLASTIC and associated logos are trademarks and/or
registered trademarks of Scholastic Inc.

Bad Guys Episode 7 Do-You-Think-He-Saurus?! first published in Australia by
Scholastic Australia, 2018
First published in the UK by Scholastic Ltd, 2019
Bad Guys Episode 8 Superbad first published in Australia by
Scholastic Australia, 2018
First published in the UK by Scholastic Ltd, 2019

This edition first published 2019

ISBN 978 1407 19338 0

A CIP catalogue record for this book
is available from the British Library.

Printed by CPI Group (UK) Ltd, Croydon, CR0 4YY
Papers used by Scholastic Children's Books are made
from wood grown in sustainable forests.

1 3 5 7 9 10 8 6 4 2

www.scholastic.co.uk

AARON BLABEY

THE BAD GUYS

EPISODE 7
DO-YOU-THINK-HE-SAURUS?!

Dave?

Tell me you're filming this?

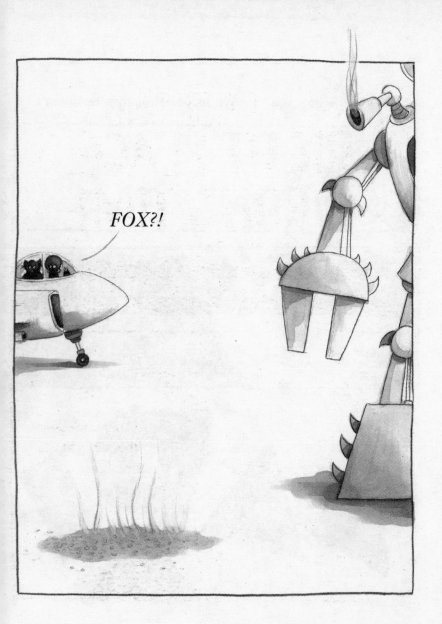

· CHAPTER 1 ·
RIGHT PLACE, WRONG TIME

65 MILLION YEARS EARLIER . . .

OK.

So, let me get this straight . . .

We were on our way to

SAVE EARTH

from an **ALIEN INVASION**

but our Escape Pod turned out to be a

TIME MACHINE

so *instead*, we've ended up in

the distant past surrounded by

DINOSAURS.

Have I got
that *right?!*

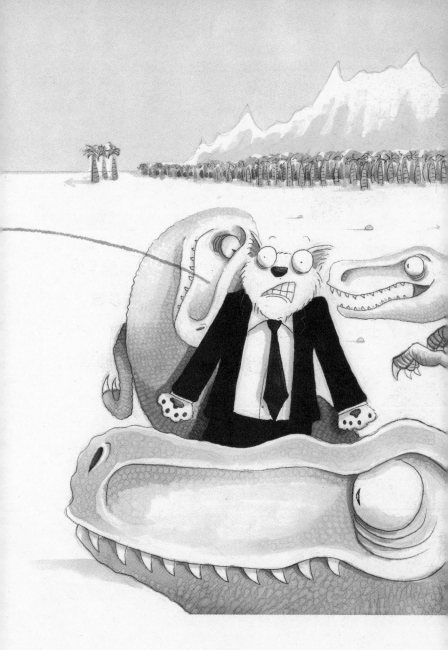

Ahhh . . . yep.
That sounds about right.

Well then—*nobody move!*
If there's one thing I know
about dinosaurs, it's this—
if you **DON'T MOVE**
they **CAN'T SEE YOU . . .**

Wolf, they can
TOTALLY
see you . . .

You'd *think* that, wouldn't you?
But, NO! I'm *completely invisible*.

Isn't it amazing?

Wolfie!
You're thinking of the
TYRANNOSAURUS REX.
These are **VELOCIRAPTORS.**
And they can TOTALLY
see you . . .

Oh, I don't think so . . .

Chico, they're looking
into your *soul*.

And it looks tasty.

You look like
soul food, bro.

Hmm, I know it
looks that way . . .
But I'm *pretty* confident
if I just keep really still
I'll be perfectly—

AARRRG GGHHH!!!

Well, amigos . . .
in Bolivia we have an old saying—

*It's better to be eaten by dinosaurs
than it is to be eaten by aliens
with butts for hands.*

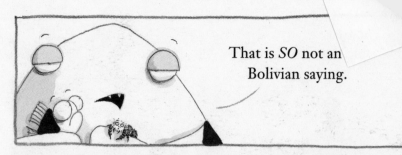

That is *SO* not an
Bolivian saying.

No.
No, it's not.

Nevertheless,
we're doomed.

I want you to know—I've
loved working with you guys.

I just feel sad we didn't really
get to save the world.

Don't feel sad yet, soldier . . .

Now, who wants a piece of me?

Snake?!

Wait a second, little buddy . . .

I've got this.

No, wait!
We can take them on TOGETHER!

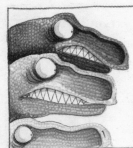

Yeah, that's right!

COME
AND
GET IT.

MR PIRANHA?
MR TARANTULA?

We'll **LEAD
THEM AWAY!**

You two need
to fix the
**TIME
MACHINE.**

EEEE!

AARGGH!

Oh sure!
We'll just
'FIX THE
TIME MACHINE'.

ARE YOU CRAZY?!

Oh chico!
Don't get me
wrong—

if anyone
can fix it,
YOU can . . .

No, no . . .
it's not that . . .

Then what?

Snake called me
'Mr Tarantula'!

I just feel really
PROUD . . .

• CHAPTER 2 •
GONE ROGUE

FOOMP!

Shhhhhhh . . .

Don't. Make.
A. Sound.

This way.
Stay close . . .

TUMBLE!

TUMBLE!

VOOSH!

FREEZE!

FOOMP!

That was close.
Now, keep low and
follow me . . .

Snake?!

Where are we going?

We have to get back to the

Time-Machine-thingy and get it working!

WE are the only ones who know

what's coming—the world is about to be

DESTROYED

BY ALIENS but we are

65 MILLION YEARS

away from the action!

WHAT ARE WE GOING TO DO?!

THIS is what we're going to do—
we're going to DEAL WITH IT.
WOLF-UP, soldier! Right now!

We're going to save the world.
Say it!

We're going to
save the world . . .

And **THIS** is how
it's going to go down . . .

Mr Shark!
YOU are going to do
what you do best . . .

I see . . .
And what *kind* of disguise
would you like?

A tree.

Done.

Man, you are good at disguises . . .

Tell me something I don't know.

Wolf!
Climb the tree!

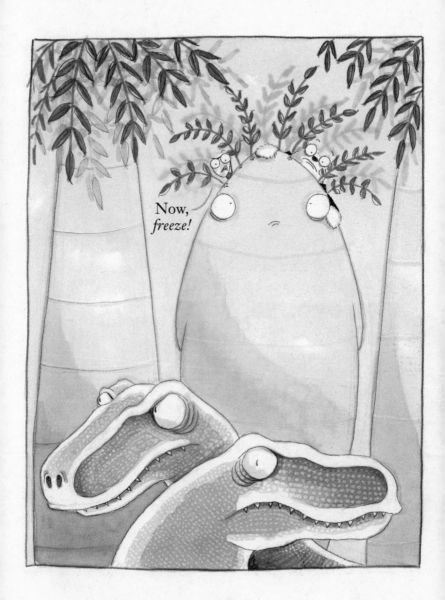

Good.
Now, Tree?
Move silently through
the jungle and get us to

HIGH GROUND.

I need to see the
lay of the land.

Yes, sir!

Who *are* you?!
And what have
you done with
Mr Snake?

CHAPTER 3

SO MANY PROBLEMS

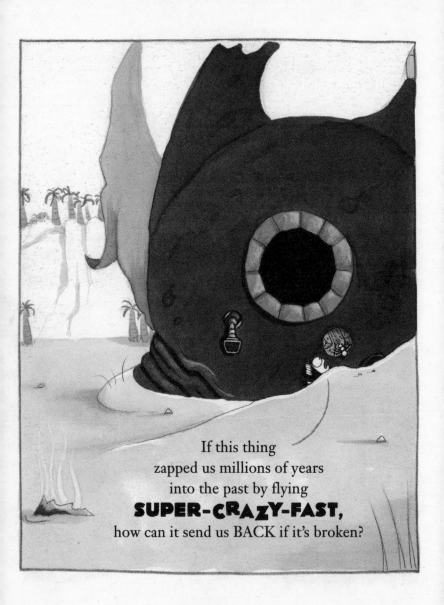

If this thing
zapped us millions of years
into the past by flying
SUPER-CRAZY-FAST,
how can it send us BACK if it's broken?

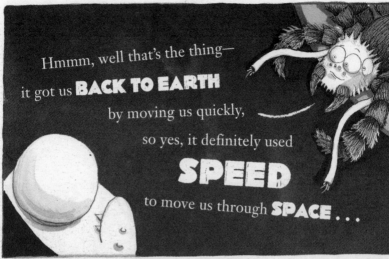

Hmmm, well that's the thing— it got us **BACK TO EARTH** by moving us quickly, so yes, it definitely used **SPEED** to move us through **SPACE**...

But what I want to do is find the part of this contraption that moved us through **TIME.**

That's a TOTALLY different thing. Don't you think?

Could you repeat the question?

Look—
this little space pod
blasted us down to Earth
from the moon and put us
exactly **WHERE** we need to be.
We're in exactly the right

PLACE.

BUT!

SPACE

TIME

It also sent us 65 million years into the **PAST.**
And that's a completely different thing.
Space. And *Time.* Two separate things, right?
So there must be something in this pod that can

OPEN A WINDOW INTO THE FUTURE.

We just need to find it, open it and *step through it.*
You hear what I'm saying?

Look!
A cloud shaped
like a pee pee . . .

So, all we need to do is identify the **TIME-TRAVEL DRIVE** . . . and if I had to guess . . .

I'd probably try to hot-wire this bit and . . .

BOOM!!

Well, *that* looks promising!

Could this be . . .
a *doorway to the future?*

Well, whatever it is, don't press *this* button.

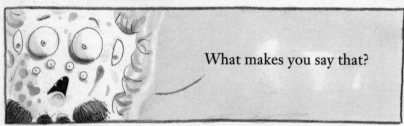

What makes you say that?

Just a feeling I have . . .

DO NOT PRESS

That **RING** . . .
Don't you think it looks like a portal?
Like a *portal through time*, perhaps?

I'll just nod my head and
hopefully you'll be struck by
lightning before you can ask me
any more stupid questions . . .

Wait—there isn't something
behind me, is there?

It's a *Tyrannosaurus rex*. Their vision IS based on movement, so if you stay completely still—

ZOOOOM!

AAARRRGGGHHH!!!

¡Ay caramba!

You're going to *move around a great deal.* THAT'S the key to success in this situation . . .

Oh.
He's still coming.
OK. Fine.

I've still got some moves.
How do you like . . .

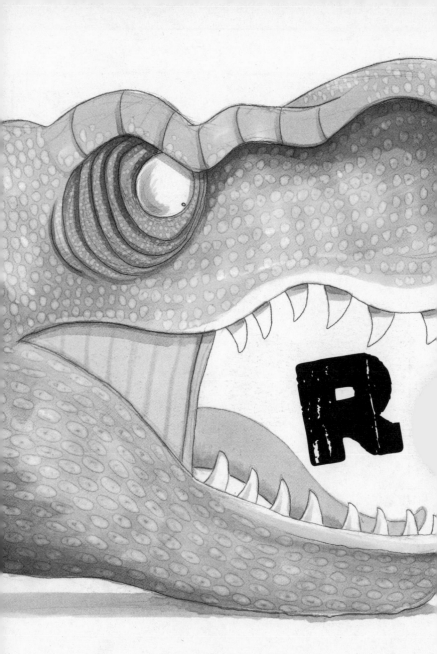

OK.
I'm in the deep poop.

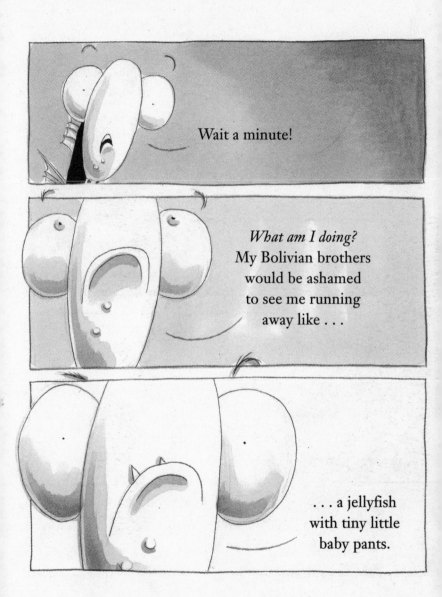

Wait a minute!

What am I doing?
My Bolivian brothers
would be ashamed
to see me running
away like . . .

. . . a jellyfish
with tiny little
baby pants.

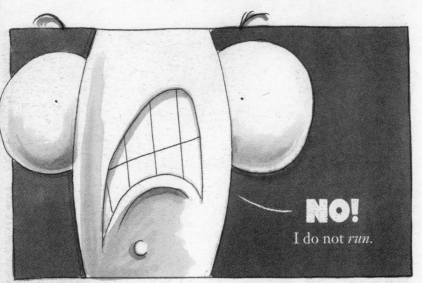

NO!
I do not *run*.

That is NOT
how I roll, señor.

I bring the THUNDER!

I bring the LIGHTNING!

I AM THE PERFECT STORM!

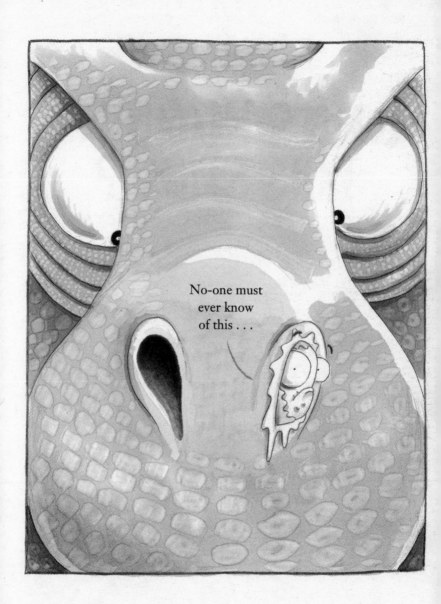

• CHAPTER 4 •
WHO'S RUNNING THIS SHOW?

What can you see?

Shhh, keep it down!
Legs is playing around
with some kind of contraption.
Where'd he get that from?

I don't see Piranha
anywhere . . .

Really?!
We should go
and look for him!
He might be
in trouble!

Oh, man.
You're right
We *are* in trouble.

It's all right though.
We'll get out of this,
I promise.
But I need you
to stay *calm*.

Listen to him, Wolfie.
He knows what he's
talking about.

You're right, Mr Shark.

And you were right before— it's almost like . . . our little team . . . has a new . . . *leader*.

Isn't it? Hehehe. Yeah.

I really am so proud of you.

Yeah, yeah.
Whatever, man.

That was *too* close.

I sure hope Mr Tarantula knows what he's doing.

· CHAPTER 5 ·
THE PORTAL

Soooo . . .
if I enter the date and
the co-ordinates, switch on
those three, bypass *that* one
and reboot *this* one . . .
Shouldn't that . . .

give me . . .

VOOF!
VOOF!
VOOF!
VOOF!
VOOF!

A VORTEX INTO ANOTHER DIMENSION!

Yeah. Pretty sure that's what it is.

Yep . . .

LOOK!

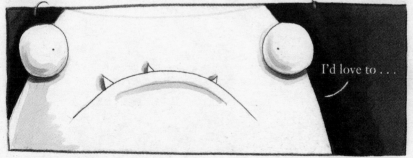

But Mr Wolf
just rang the

**DINNER
BELL!**

RUN!

No, Wolf! Wait a minute!

Aw, man,
I'm not wearing
any pants . . . .

Look out!

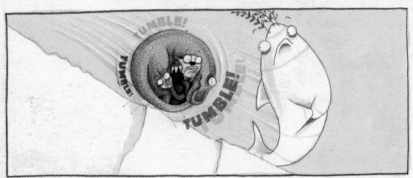

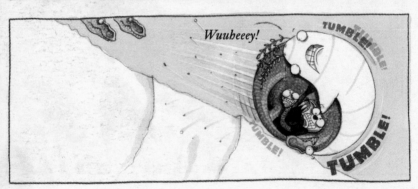

Wuuheeey!

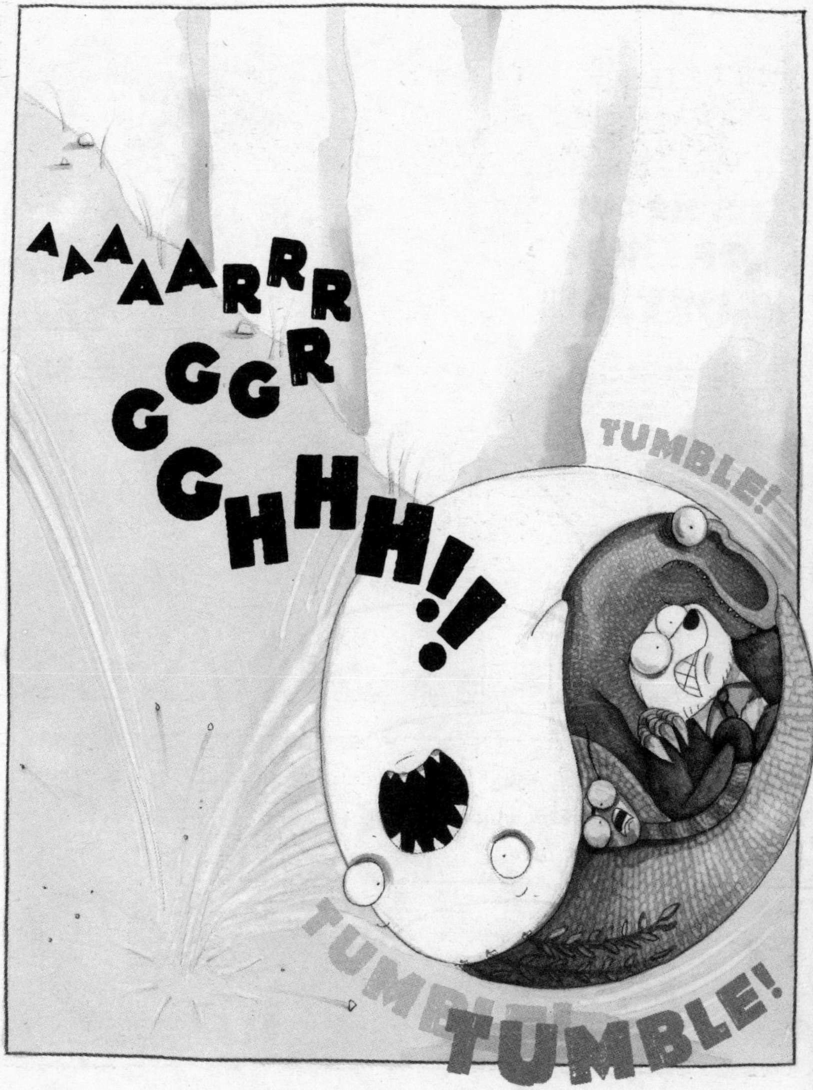
AAAAARRRR
GGGR
GHHH!!
TUMBLE!
TUMBLE!
TUMBLE!

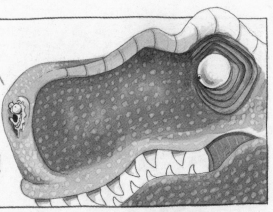

I'VE HAD
ENOUGH
OF THIS!
**LET ME OUT
OF THIS
NOSTRIL!**

PIRANHA!
Is that you?!

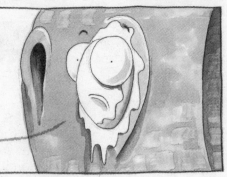

No! No! It's not me!
This is just a *dream*, chico!
*I am not stuck in
a dinosaur's nostril.*

You **NEVER
SAW THIS,**
understand?

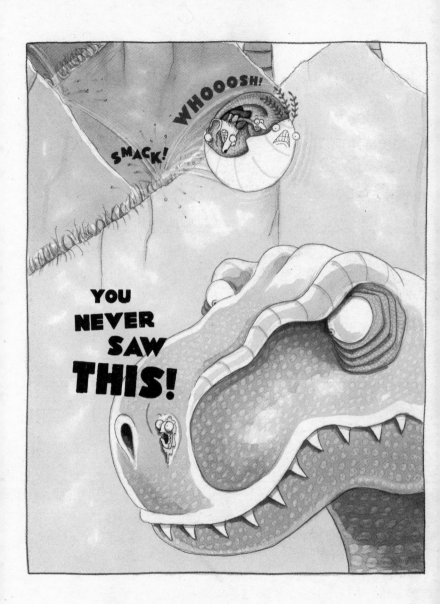

Piranha!
It IS you!

Everyone,
into the vortex!

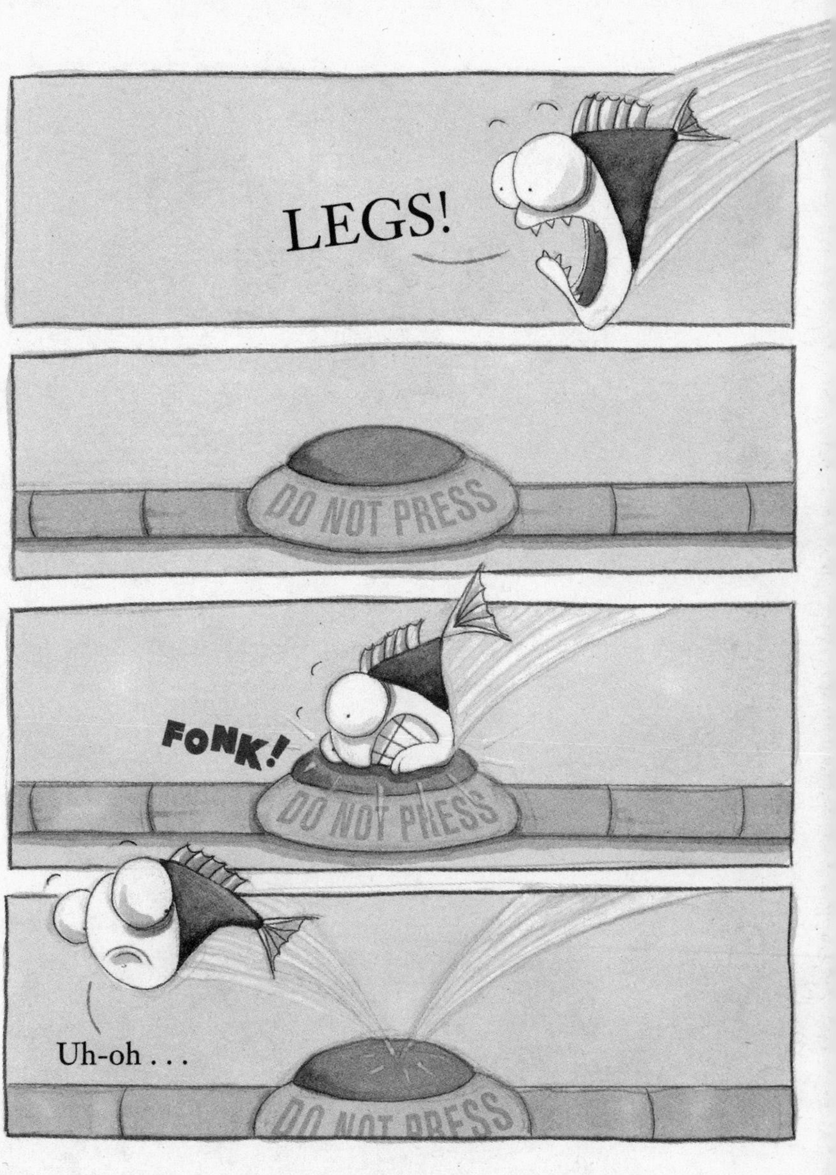
LEGS!
DO NOT PRESS
FONK!
DO NOT PRESS
Uh-oh . . .
DO NOT PRESS

They jumped into that swirly circle! Everybody, follow me!

Hey— what happens if a **VELOCIRAPTOR** follows us into that thing?

Aw, don't worry about that.

It'll be fine . . .

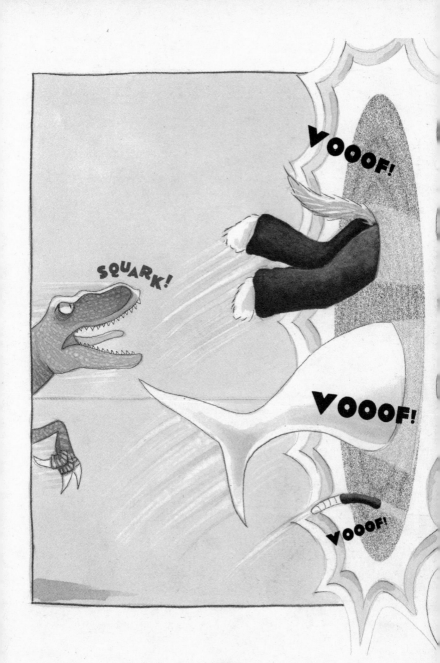

FIZZZZZ...

· CHAPTER 6 ·
ONE WAY TICKET TO WEIRD TOWN

WOW!

This is so beautiful!

And so *peaceful* . . .

Hmmm.

I wonder how the others are doing.

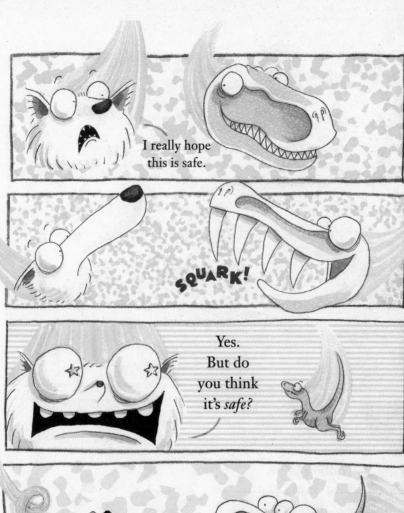

Do I look strange to you?

In what way?

I don't know.
I just don't feel
like myself . . .

Does anyone else feel

AWESOME?

What a pleasant journey.
Dude, that was just delightful.

But hey!
Look over there . . .
That looks just like . . .

· CHAPTER 7 ·
BACK TO THE . . .
YOU KNOW

Mr Wolf!
You're alive!

Agent Fox!
There's **ALIENS!**
I mean, Marmalade is . . .
I mean, THEY'RE COMING!

Mr Wolf . . .
They're
already
here.

Oh no.

What just **HAPPENED?!**
I feel WEIRD, chicos.

I feel AWESOME.
Does anyone else feel
AWESOME?

How about you?
Do you feel—

My goodness, what a *kerfuffle!*

I'm terribly sorry, but we've not been formally introduced . . .

· CHAPTER 8 ·
HUH?!

ARRRRGGHHH!

It's *TALKING!*

**RUN!
FOLLOW ME!**

Heavens!
That little chap was
certainly in a hurry!

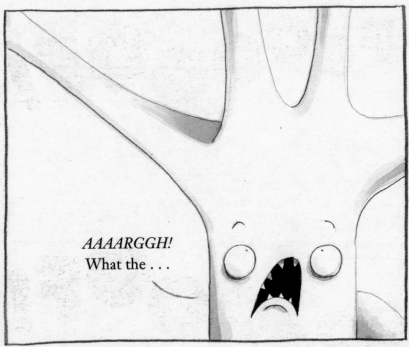

AAAARGGH!
What the . . .

SHAKE!

SHAKE!

SHAKE!

SHAKE!

No no no no no!

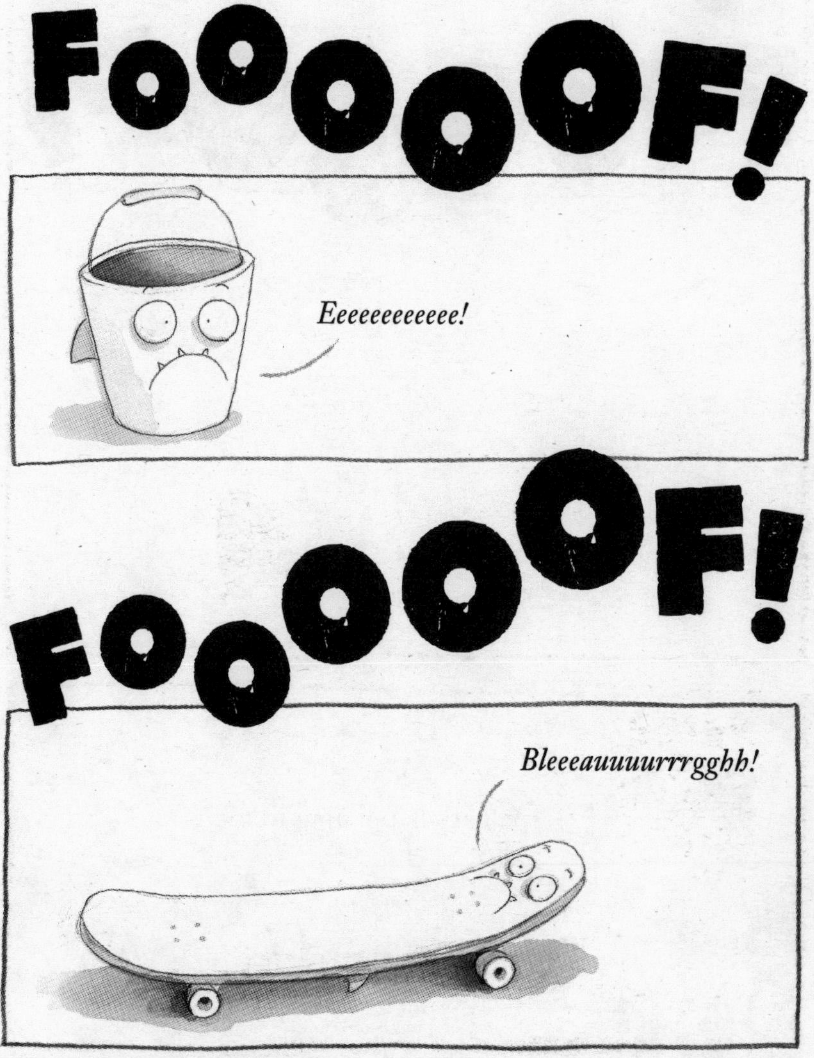
FOOOOOF!
Eeeeeeeeeeee!
FOOOOOF!
Bleeeauuuurrrgghh!

FOOOOOF!

Bwah-hahaharrrgh!

What's happening to me?!

Mr Shark . . .
You're shape-shifting.

You think *that's* cool?

Check this out . . .

SHUDDER!
SHUDDER!

Guys, I think Mr Snake is lifting a car . . .
with his **MIND.**

Mr Wolf?
I feel a little scared.
What's going on here, man?

I'm not sure,
buddy.

But if I had to
guess . . .

I'd say we've
got ourselves
some . . .

SUPE

MAIL

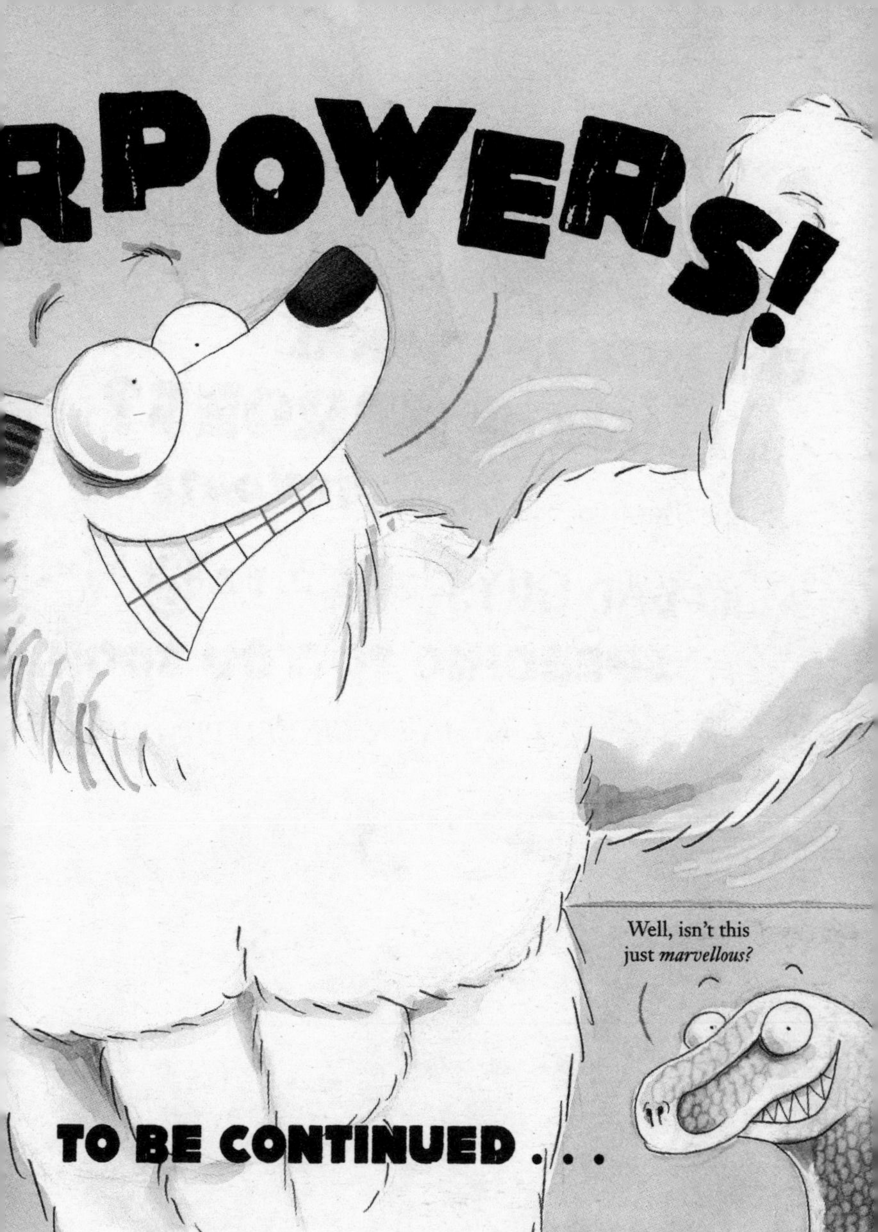
RPOWERS!
Well, isn't this just *marvellous?*
TO BE CONTINUED . . .

SUPER POWERS?! Who saw THAT coming?!

THE BAD GUYS might have got an upgrade,

but does that *guarantee* them a place in

THE INTERNATIONAL
LEAGUE OF HEROES?

Nope. But they will be holding **TRYOUTS...**

the **BAD GUYS** EPISODE **8**
SPEEDING TO YOU SOON.

LIKE AN ENHANCED PIRANHA.

The following broadcast was picked up by satellite, while being beamed from Earth into Deep Space . . .

KEEPING UP WITH

KDJFLOER HGCOINW ERUHCGLE IRWFHEKLW JFHXALHW!

PILOT EPISODE
*The Glamorous Life of
Dr Rupert Marmalade*

Hiiiiiiii everyone!
This is soooooooooo exciting!
My very own
REALITY TV SHOW!
I could just *die*.

But what's that, you say?
Who IS this disgusting
CUTE and **CUDDLY**
little creature calling himself
DR RUPERT MARMALADE?
Well, I've only got one thing
to say about that . . .

ZZZZZ ZZZZZZ**ZZIP!**

I know you've *all* been wondering
what I've been up to since I left
our planet with an **ARMY** and a fleet of
WARSHIPS and all I can say is it's been
ONE BIG PARTY!
You have NO idea . . .

WOOT!
WOOT!

I've been on an

INTERGALACTIC SHOPPING SPREE

and I was like
*'OMG, Earth? Yes, please!
I'll TAKE IT!'*

I just *had* to have it.

I've worked SO hard to make
it my own, you know?

I really wanted to, like, personalise it
and make a real statement with it.

I think it's just so 'me'.

And all the little creatures who lived here are mine now too!

I RULE WITHOUT MERCY.

But at the same time,
I'm *super fun* to be around.
You know what I mean?
I'm SO complicated.

10 THINGS I LOOOOOVE!

1. Having my own planet

2. Showing no pity

3. Chocolate sprinkles

4. Feeling the fear of millions

5. Leading my invading army to victory

6. Annihilating my enemies

7. Cheese sticks

8. Intergalactic domination

9. Watching my enemies lose all hope

10. Skinny jeans

10 THINGS I TOTALLY HATE

1. Being called **CUTE**

2. Being called **CUDDLY**

3. Being called **CUTE AND CUDDLY**

4. Being called anything that implies I'm **CUTE AND CUDDLY** without actually saying it

5. Wolves, Sharks, Snakes, Piranhas and Foxes
(It's an Earth thing. But don't worry. It's TOTALLY under control.)

6. Body hair (ugh)

7. Running out of cheese sticks

8. Books that end with the words 'To be continued . . .'

9. The happiness of others

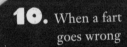

10. When a fart goes wrong

My *hopes and dreams?*

Well, I've already accomplished so much, you know?
I'm rich. I'm *gorgeous.* I have a planet of my own,
with a side order of **ABSOLUTE POWER.**

I've got it all.

So . . . I guess my dream is
to wake up tomorrow being just as
PERFECT AS I AM TODAY.

I think that's something
we can ALL relate to.

And to everyone watching back on my **BEAUTIFUL HOME PLANET,** I'd like to send you this message . . .

For all the **INSPIRATION** I give you—

You're welcome.

Now, if you'll excuse me,
I have a busy day ahead of me—
I'm producing a movie version
of *the story of my life.*

It's called

HE'S JUST AMAZEBALLS.

I wrote the screenplay.
It's even better than it sounds.
We've hired some good-looking kid
to play me, but personally I don't think
anyone will have what it takes.

QUIET
ON SET

JUSTIN
BEAVER

DIRECTOR
STEVEN
SEALBERG

AARON BLABEY

THE BAD GUYS

EPISODE 8   SUPERBAD

What did you say to me?

Get in line?!

DON'T YOU KNOW WHO I AM?!

Well, if he *does* know, honey,
he doesn't seem to care . . .

MOVE!

LET THOSE CITIZENS GO!

CHAPTER 1

IDIOTS ASSEMBLE

It's the
GOOD GUYS CLUB!

Ah yes!
But we are developing a
better name that will sound
much cooler, señorita . . .

Get on with it, man . . .

Yes! Of course!
You've messed with the wrong
planet, hermanos.

SUPER SPEED . . .

Oh, man.
He did it again.
He, like, ran straight
into that thing . . .

Yeah, well, aliens?
I bet you weren't counting on . . .

THIS!

FoOOOOF!

Oh, no, no . . .
wait a minute . . .
hold that thought . . .

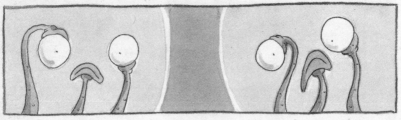

Aw, this is just embarrassing . . .

NO! These antics
have all been a
cunning trick to
distract you from
THIS!

FOOOOOF!

Oooh.
My bad.
Sorry, man.

It's . . . all . . . good . . .

That's ENOUGH!
We're not playing around
ANYMORE!

Let me show you
WHAT WE'RE
MADE OF!

Dude, you are SO
naked right now . . .

Mr Wolf!
WHAT ARE YOU DOING?!

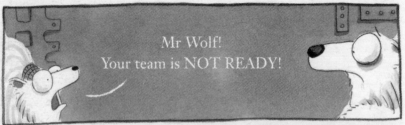

Mr Wolf!
Your team is NOT READY!

What makes you say that?

I know your hearts
are in the right place,
but you need our help.

When we're finished with you,
you'll be ready to take on

ANYTHING.

Good Guys Club?
Meet . . .

• CHAPTER 2 •
THE LEAGUE

MEET
THE TEAM...

AGENT FOX

NAME: CLASSIFIED

PERSONAL HISTORY: CLASSIFIED

MASTER of SPYCRAFT

MASTER of MARTIAL ARTS

FLUENT in 14 LANGUAGES

PREFERRED VEHICLE: ANY

AGENT KITTY KAT

NAME: CLASSIFIED

PERSONAL HISTORY: CLASSIFIED

MASTER of MARTIAL ARTS

DOCTOR of MEDICINE

PILOT: FIRST CLASS

PREFERRED VEHICLE: AIRCRAFT

AGENT HOGWILD

NAME: CLASSIFIED

PERSONAL HISTORY: CLASSIFIED

DEMOLITIONS EXPERT

COMBAT SPECIALIST

PREFERRED VEHICLE:
MOTORCYCLE

AGENT DOOM

NAME: CLASSIFIED

PERSONAL HISTORY: CLASSIFIED

COMPUTER HACKING GENIUS

DOCTOR of BIOLOGY, CHEMISTRY, PHYSICS, BIO-ENGINEERING + PHILOSOPHY

Meh.

AGENT SHORTFUSE

NAME: CLASSIFIED

PERSONAL HISTORY: CLASSIFIED

SPECIAL SKILLS: CLASSIFIED

That was so awesome.

I've seen better.

That video was so professional.

Why are we even here?

Because Fox has this crazy idea that you have potential.

But personally . . .

I don't have high hopes.

· CHAPTER 3 ·
WHAT'S GOING ON

Welcome to our
SECRET HEADQUARTERS.
Now you know a little bit about us,
so let's talk about **YOU.**

Mr Wolf, Mr Snake, Mr Shark and Mr Piranha—
the International League of Heroes is
well aware of your recent work and
we've all been briefed on your . . .
NEW TALENTS.

Hey, Wolf.
While we listen,
go and get me a
MUFFIN.

Get yourself a muffin.

No, you didn't
hear me.
*YOU WILL GET
ME A MUFFIN.*

I will get you a muffin . . .

I'd also like to introduce my team to another very special member of the Good Guys Club—

LEGS!

Legs?
Are you OK?
You don't seem
your usual,
cheerful self.

Huh?
Yeah.
I'm fine.
Just FINE.

He likes to be called Mr Tarantula!

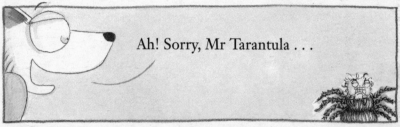

Ah! Sorry, Mr Tarantula . . .

Yeah, yeah,
WHATEVER!

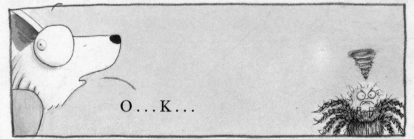

O . . . K . . .

It's the weirdest thing . . .
I just got you a muffin.

Aw, thanks!

And finally, the . . . er . . . newest
member of the Good Guys Club—
MILTON.

And yes, in case you're wondering,
Milton *does* appear to be a **DINOSAUR**
from the Cretaceous period . . .

A dinosaur with an IQ of **512**.

According to my tests, he's easily the **MOST INTELLIGENT BEING ON THE FACE OF THE EARTH**.

Does anyone want to explain that?

It's kind of creeping me out . . .

Oh you're making me blush, dear lady—*really!*

What's a few hundred IQ points between friends? I'm just thrilled to be involved, and I must say, you all seem *lovely*.

Who'd care for a cup of tea?

Yep, that just happened.

Seriously, am I the only one creeped out by him?

Sooooo, obviously something highly unusual happened to all of you when you passed through that **VORTEX.**

Milton became **HYPER-INTELLIGENT . . .**

I really like her. She's *delightful*, don't you think?

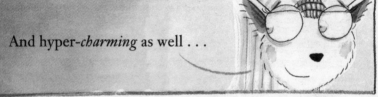

And hyper-*charming* as well . . .

On the other hand, Mr Piranha has

SUPER SPEED.

Mr Shark can

SHAPE-SHIFT.

Mr Snake has rather remarkable

MIND POWERS . . .

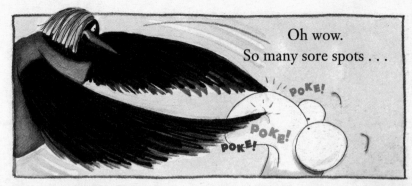

Oh wow.
So many sore spots . . .

POKE!
POKE!
POKE!

Yeah, yeah.
Run away, 'Mr Remarkable'.
I've got my eye on you.

And as for
MR WOLF . . .

Aw, he's just a good old-fashioned **NUDIST!**
You looked FINE out there today,
baaaybeeee . . .

Keep it nice, Agent Hogwild.

As we all know, Mr Wolf has

SUPER STRENGTH.

Hey! Why are you holding a trumpet, chico?

Now ain't YOU a cutey . . .

Gulp!

Unfortunately though, there's a **PROBLEM.**
Other than Milton, none of you are able to fully **CONTROL** your powers . . .

I'VE GOT POWERS!
I DO! AND I
CAN CONTROL THEM!
LOOK! I'VE GOT
CRAZY SPIDER POWERS. . .

Ahhh . . . I think that's just called **'BEING A SPIDER'** isn't it?

Yeah, buddy. It kind of is.

But that's why we LOVE YOU, chico! You're just the **SAME OLD MR TARANTULA!**

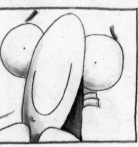

WHY DIDN'T I GET SUPERPOWERS?!

Ohhh, THAT'S why you're grouchy . . .

I'M NOT GROUCHY!

Dear boy, it pains me to see you like this.

If I *had* to hazard a guess as to why you weren't transformed like the rest of us, I'd suggest it *might* be because you passed through the vortex **BEFORE** your Bolivian friend switched on the **ENHANCEMENT DRIVE . . .**

HOW *DARE* YOU!
I didn't switch on ANYTHING!

Are you certain?
It was probably marked
'DO NOT PRESS' or
something like that . . .

Look!
A cloud shaped
like a peanut . . .

You like peanuts?
Why don't we go out tonight and
get a whole crate of peanuts?

That sounds like **FUN.**
I bet you're a
good dancer, too.
Wanna go dancin'?

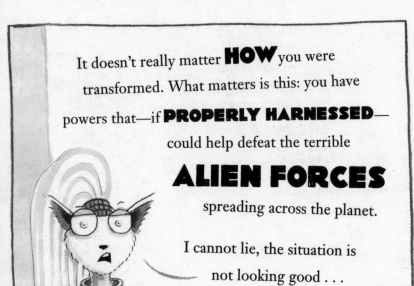

It doesn't really matter **HOW** you were transformed. What matters is this: you have powers that—if **PROPERLY HARNESSED**—could help defeat the terrible

ALIEN FORCES

spreading across the planet.

I cannot lie, the situation is not looking good . . .

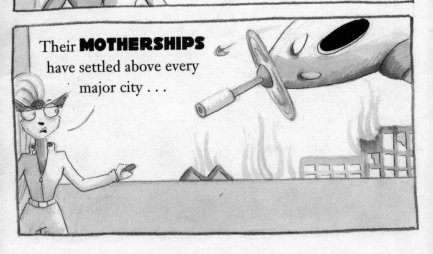

Their **MOTHERSHIPS** have settled above every major city . . .

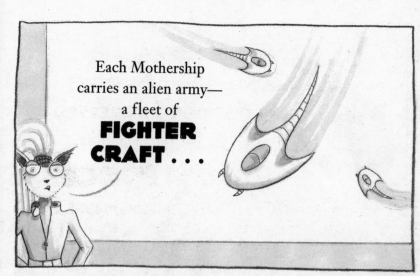

Each Mothership
carries an alien army—
a fleet of
**FIGHTER
CRAFT . . .**

and a legion of
**ROBOT WAR
MACHINES**
used by the aliens
on the ground.

The aliens are able to

CHANGE THEIR SIZE AT WILL.

They can be gigantic one minute and then shrink down to

fit inside the helmet of a **WAR MACHINE.**

That's how **MARMALADE**

disguised himself as a guinea pig.

They are HIGHLY ADVANCED.

They are HOSTILE.

And they are **EVERYWHERE.**

Well in that case, I'd better put my **ENORMOUS BRAIN** to work and come up with a **PLAN.**

BUT!
I'll need an assistant!
And there's only one name
at the top of my list—
MR TARANTULA,
I need you!
I suspect you're more
important to our survival
than you think . . .

Yeah, OK,
*what*ever . . .

Goodness!
I've just realised
you are entirely
without trousers!

Yeah, well, get over it . . .

And as for the rest of you . . .

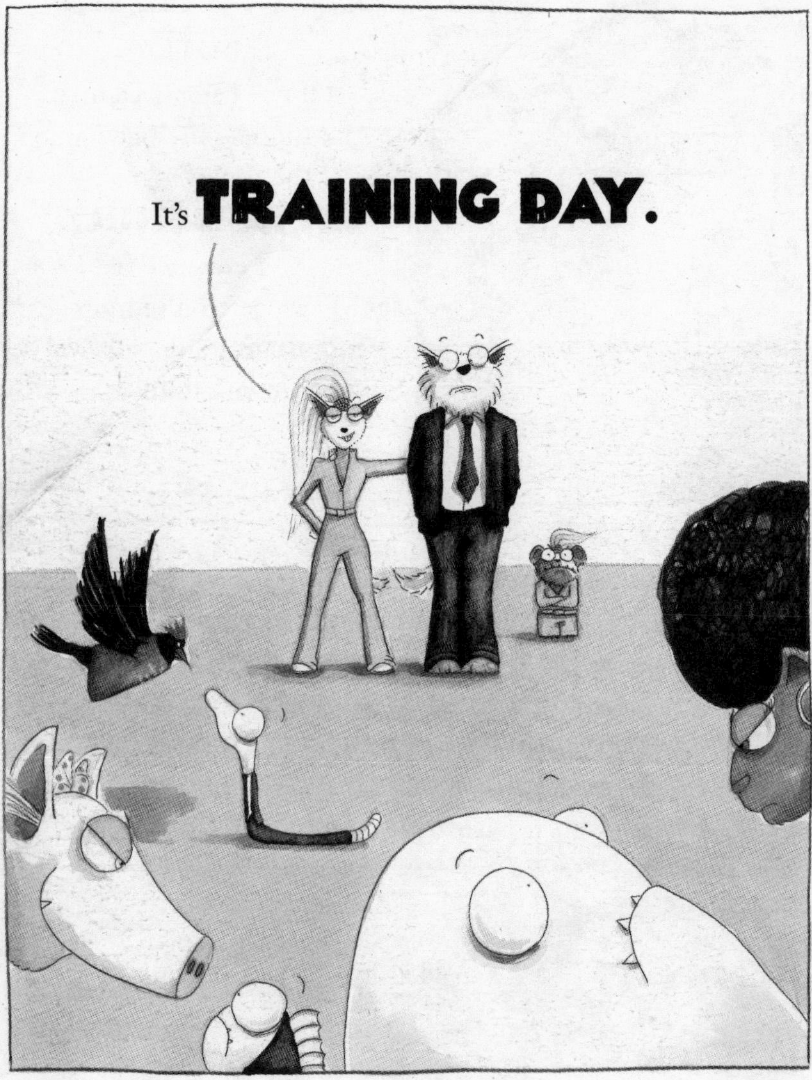
It's TRAINING DAY.

· CHAPTER 4 ·
BE A TEACUP

Lesson One—
DON'T ANNOY ME.

But can you be a teacup . . .

when it matters?

SSSSSSSSSSS!

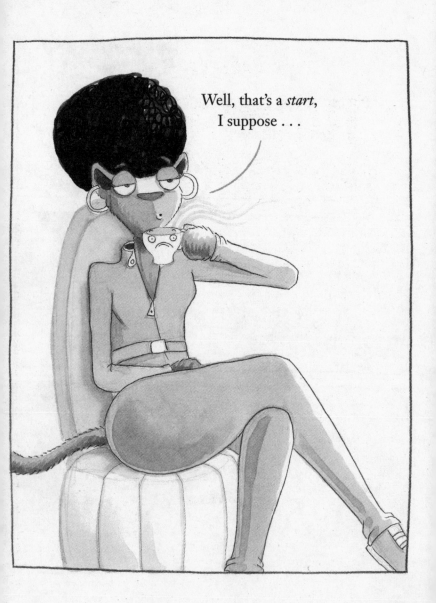

CHAPTER 5

TURN! TURN! TURN!

What's going on here?!
Why are we in this
TINY METAL ROOM?

Well . . . we're
going to play
a **GAME.**

Oh . . . OK . . . I like games.
What kind of game?

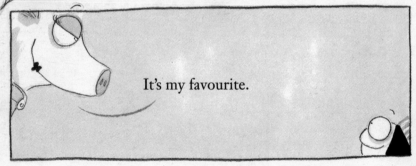

It's my favourite.

 Really? What's it called?

 **HOGWILD CHASE**

 What does that involve . . ?

GO!

WAIT! I'M NOT READY!

FAAAAZOOOOM!

AAAAIIIIEEEE!

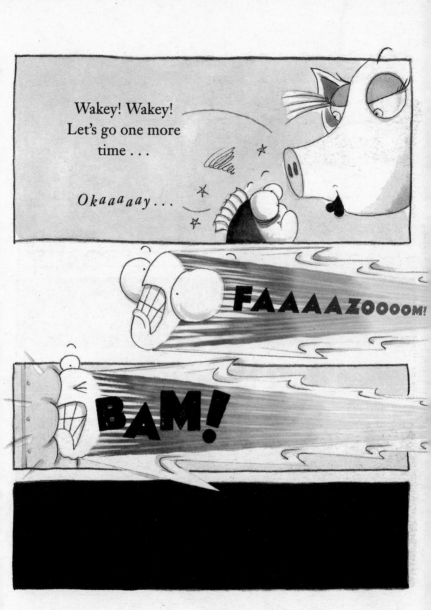

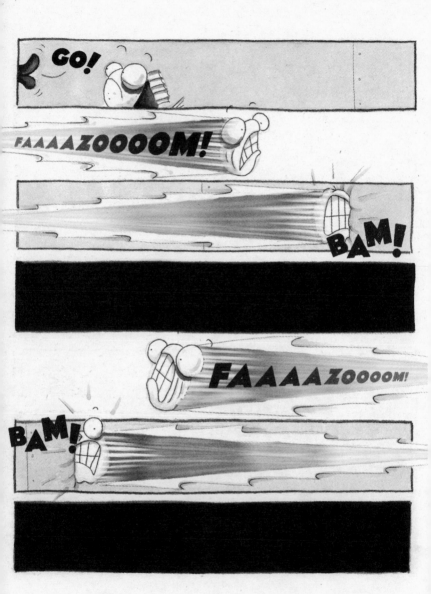

Listen, baby, I could do this ALL day.

But we're in a bit of a rush, and you
have to stop crashing into walls,
so we need to take this to the

NEXT LEVEL . . .

Ready?

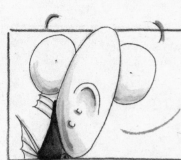

But I'll be a little fish-kebab!

You think I'd let that
happen to you?
I *believe* in you, sweet cheeks.
All you have to do is

TURN.

I KNOW you can do it.

GO!

· CHAPTER 6 ·

THE BAD GIRLS

Yeah.
Well, I've seen better.

Oh sure.

Anyone can lift a **FRIDGE,**

a **CHAINSAW** and a

SECRET AGENT

off the ground using only their

MIND . . .

 So . . . why don't we get Agent Fox to sing a little opera . . .

 And let's start up that chainsaw . . .

GRRRRING!
GRRRRRING!!

 YAWN

Oh, c'mon!
That was *awesome!*

Hey Fox? Can you take over?
Mr Remarkable's cheap tricks
are really bumming me out.

Why do you think we call her **'AGENT DOOM'**?

Why does she have to be so **NEGATIVE?**

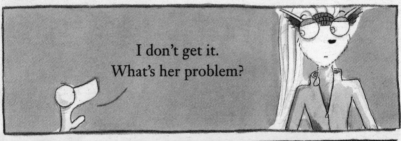

I don't get it. What's her problem?

She's just pushing your buttons, Mr Snake. To see how you'll react.

Yeah, I get it.

YOU SUPER-SHINY-HERO-LADIES

think we're NOTHING don't you?

We're just a bunch of dirty crooks, right?

You don't think we've got what it takes.

None of you do.

But let me tell you something—

You don't know me AT ALL.

YOU KNOW

NOTHING

ABOUT ME.

Where I come from,
they **HUNT** foxes, Mr Snake. For fun.
Because they think we're worthless,
dirty thieves who don't deserve to live.

When I was young . . .

I lost everything.

Well, they told her early on that she couldn't be on the playground with the other kids because she had a **WILD SIDE.**

Eventually, that made her pretty angry too.

And **AGENT HOGWILD**
was *told* her whole life she was bad.
So guess what?
She started *acting* like she was bad.

AGENT DOOM
was picked on every single day
for being a 'creepy weirdo' . . .

And nobody even
wanted to go near
AGENT SHORTFUSE.
Ever.

But then, somehow, we found each other.

And we made a pact.

We decided to take all our hurt and our anger and our fear and turn it all into something **GOOD**.

Instead of trying to hurt those who'd hurt us, we started trying to **PROTECT THOSE WHO CAN'T PROTECT THEMSELVES.**

So, don't you see, Mr Snake?

We *are* you.

· CHAPTER 7 ·
THE FINAL EXAM

Hey, why don't I get a training session?

Because all you need are these.

They'll stretch as much as you need, Major Big Butt.

SUPER-STRETCH

Put them away for now though, Mr Wolf. You guys have something you need to do first . . .

MOMENTS LATER . . .

EEEEEEEE!

Huh?

This is your
FINAL TRAINING EXERCISE.
It's simple—*put Agent Shortfuse in the box.*
Good luck, gentlemen.

Oh man, I was worried
there for a second.
OK, Agent Shortfuse,
we can do this the
EASY WAY or—

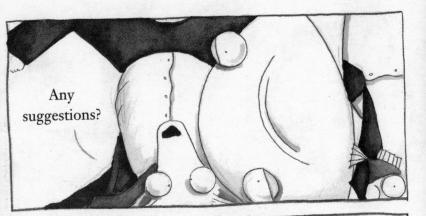

Any suggestions?

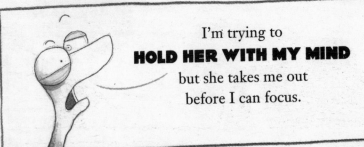

I'm trying to
HOLD HER WITH MY MIND
but she takes me out
before I can focus.

She's too fast and too strong.
None of us can take her **ALONE.**

In your face,
Shortfuse!
You can't catch me!

And
while he
distracts
her . . .

I've got her . . .
but, geeeeeez . . . not for long . . .

And the best way to
surprise her is from . . .

BAM!

WHISTLE!
WHISTLE!

Gentlemen?
YOU'RE READY.

· CHAPTER 8 ·
A MARVELLOUS PLAN

 OPERATION TARANTULA

Ladies and gentlemen, I have developed a **PLAN** to give us the upper hand in this struggle against the Alien Forces. I call it—*Operation Tarantula!*

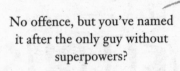

No offence, but you've named it after the only guy without superpowers?

Really?

WE don't have 'superpowers'. You got a problem with THAT?!

It's elementary! Mr Tarantula is the **ONLY** individual in the room capable of **OPERATING AN ALIEN SPACECRAFT,** is he not?

That's not true. I could *totally* do it.

And **OPERATION DOOM** would sound totes cooler.

Hmmm. But are you small enough to sneak into the control deck of the Mothership **WITHOUT BEING NOTICED?**

NO! YOU ARE *NOT!* The **ONLY** way we can stop this invasion is to take charge of a Mothership and turn it against them. Therefore! The mission is to **SNEAK MR TARANTULA ON BOARD,** any way we can.

But what about all the aliens **ON BOARD?** Who will protect Legs? He can't go in there alone . . .

Oh no, dear boy. He won't be alone . . .

NOD! **NOD!**

Yeah . . . that could work.

Sounds good to me.

MY TEAM will take on the aliens here on the *ground*. We'll keep them off you as long as we can.

Mr Wolf?
Your team needs to get

AGENT SHORTFUSE
and **MR TARANTULA**
onto that **MOTHERSHIP.**

· CHAPTER 9 ·

BIG
TROUBLE

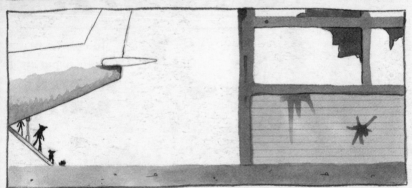

This is it,
Mr Wolf.

Are you OK?

I . . .
I just feel a little . . .

You'll do *great*.

MR WOLF?!

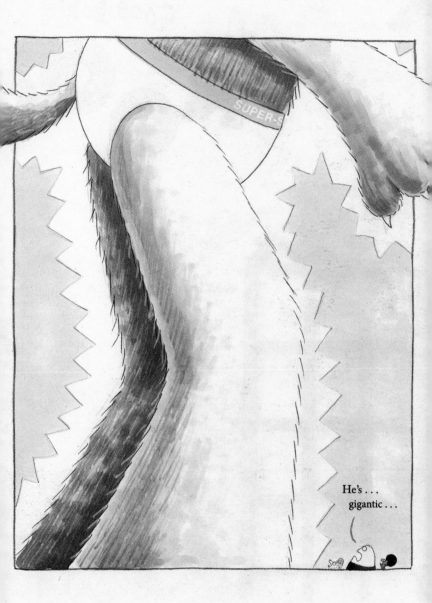

He's . . .
gigantic . . .

TO BE CONTINUED . . .

The Three Little Pigs were *right?!*

the BAD GUYS EPISODE **9**

COMING SOON...

TO DESTROY YOUR TOWN.